Uncle Tea's Big Jump

Written by Jill Eggleton
Illustrated by Brent Chambers

The people in the book

Uncle Ted

The twins

Mom and Dad

The river in the book

When the twins got home from school, they saw Uncle Ted's truck.

"Uncle Ted's here," they shouted.

They loved it when Uncle Ted came.
He was funny.
He had big teeth that went…

CLACK!

CLACK!

CLACK!

Uncle Ted had a bag of presents.

He had slippers for Mom. They looked like duck feet.

He had a hat for Dad with big ears like an elephant.

And he had sunglasses for the twins.

The kids are...?

After dinner, Uncle Ted was reading the paper.

"Look at this," he said.

BIG JUMP

Come and do the **BIG JUMP**.

You will LOVE it!

Not for kids.

"I'm going to do that big jump," said Uncle Ted.

"WOW," said the twins.

"It's not for kids," he said. "But you can come and watch."

The kids are...

too small?   Yes? No?

too old?   Yes? No?

Uncle Ted waved to the twins.

"**This is fun,**" he shouted.

The woman said,

"ONE! TWO! THREE! JUMP!"

Uncle Ted looked down. He looked down again. And then he…

Uncle Ted went...

BOING, BOING, BOING,

up and **down,** **up** and **down!**

Uncle Ted had his mouth open and **oops...** his big teeth fell out!

Uncle Ted is...?

When Uncle Ted came back to the truck, he looked very funny.

"Where are your teeth?" said the twins.

Uncle Ted laughed.

"My teeth fell out," he said. "They will be in the river!"

The teeth will be...

on the water?

under the water?

The twins and Uncle Ted went back home.
On the way, Uncle Ted gave them oranges to eat.

When they got home, the twins jumped out of the truck.

They ran inside shouting, "Uncle Ted's teeth fell out. Uncle Ted's teeth fell out."

Mom will...

laugh?

cry?

But Uncle Ted said, "No they didn't, LOOK!"

They all laughed and laughed.

"Are you going to do a big jump again?" said Mom.

"No," said Uncle Ted. "I'm not jumping again. My eyes will fall out!"

Advertisements

Lost

Big white teeth

Phone Uncle Ted

555-2793

The twins have lost their sunglasses.
What will you put in the ad?
Where will it go?

a sock

the twins

Sunglasses

Phone

Lost

Phone the doctor

555-2498

Word Bank

bag

ears

elephant

ladder

oranges

paper

presents

river

slippers

sunglasses

teeth

truck